THE DRABBLE

ADVENT

CALENDAR

a 100 word story each
day until Christmas

THE DRABBLE ADVENT CALENDAR

LINTUSEN PRESS

© 2021 Lintusen Press
Ebook ISBN 978-1-989642-29-0
Paperback ISBN 978-1-989642-28-3

This book uses Canadian spelling.

Lintusen Press
PO Box 10019
Salmon Arm, BC
Canada V1E 3B9

ABOUT
THE DRABBLE
ADVENT CALENDAR

A drabble is a literary *amuse-bouche*. It's precisely 100 words, a perfect miniature snack of story to enjoy.

As kids, do you remember the fun of chocolate advent calendars leading up to Christmas Day? Each morning we eagerly anticipated a taste of something special, a little treat amid the bustle of the season.

So here is a literary count-down for you: twenty-five micro-stories relating to northern winter and the holiday season, in a variety of genres. They're geared to adults, but not unsuitable for younger family members.

Turn the page daily to savour a brief escape into a holiday moment.

MEDITATIONS FROM A TREE WELL, UPSIDE DOWN

Shawn L Bird

I am suspended by my skis, arms pinned.
I'm helpless.
I know the stats: tree wells are the leading cause of skiers' deaths.
What a stupid way to die! I'd thought. *Has to be a joke.*
Such irony.
Seconds count, but I'm stuck.
Blood rushing to my head will soon cause black-out.
If the bindings release, I'll fall.
If I hit my head, I'll break my neck.
If snow collapses over me, I will suffocate.
I'm going to freeze.
I'm waiting for death.
Then, in the distance, muffled noises: barking, shouts.
Tumbling snow tickles my neck.
"Good dog!" someone calls.

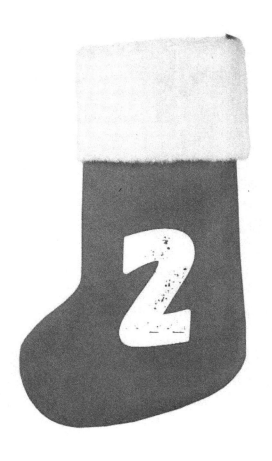

TYPOGRAPHICAL ERROR

Chris McMahen

As she walked through the airport, Marlene had her suspicions something wasn't quite right.

The flight had taken much longer than expected. When she stepped off the plane, the blast of humid tropical air didn't feel like Saskatoon in December. And why were so many people speaking Spanish?

She checked her boarding pass once more and discovered she'd made a terrible mistake. Her Christmas holiday plans had been radically altered by a simple typographical error when she brought her ticket.

Instead of 'Saskatoon,' she'd typed 'Acapulco!' What a silly thing to do. She really should be more careful next year.

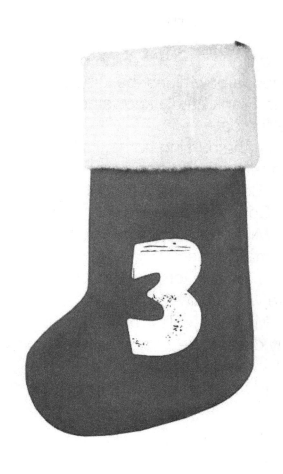

THE PRICELESS GIFT

Finnian Burnett

Mildred sighs. The wrapping paper is lopsided; a bow hides the lumps. It doesn't matter. Frank barely knows her name, let alone the date.

At the nursing home, her husband's sitting up—a good sign.

"Bobby visited today," he says.

Bobby died twelve years ago.

Mildred kisses him. "I've brought you a Christmas present."

"I got one for you, too." He hands her a note with a bow.

Mildred reads Frank's laboured scrawl, barely discernible. "My present to you. All my love for the rest of my life."

In this moment, he's lucid. "The rest of my life," he says.

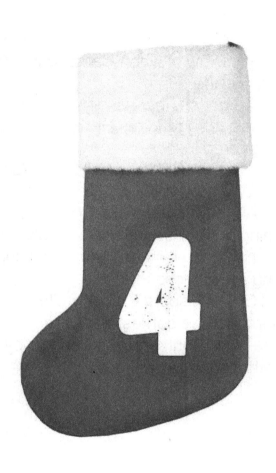

ICE FAIRIES

Lee F. Patrick

Being sick is awful when Carrie wants to be playing outside.

She goes to her window to see if her friends are tobogganing. Her windows seem to be covered in lace.

"Daddy, look!" she calls, wonder in her voice. "What did this?"

"Ah, aren't you a lucky girl," he says, wrapping an arm around her. "You've had a visit from the ice fairies! They paint windows to bring joy to those inside."

"Oh!" whispers Carrie, while her father ponders that the darkest days are those of the heart and soul, and what brings joy, also brings hope for better days.

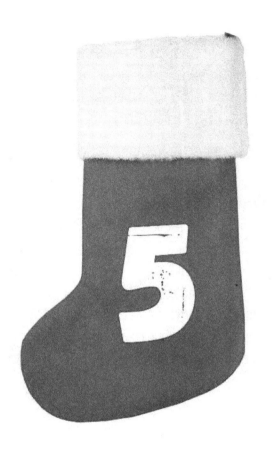

IT'S ALL DOWNHILL FROM HERE

Carol Parchewsky

"It's easy to cross country ski," they said. "Strap on the skis and settle into the tracks."

"Follow along," they said as their arms pumped, poles launching them faster along the trail.

No one said to watch out for animals that ran across the trail.

No one said what the magic words were to make the elderly stubborn rabbit sleeping on the trail at the midpoint of the first hill move.

No one said there would be hills.

No one said balletic gymnastic movements would occur when your skis left the ruts during downward acceleration.

Until I screamed it.

Loudly.

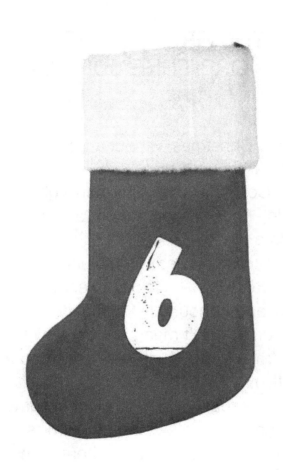

BEGIN AS YOU WANT TO GO ON: THE FIRST CHRISTMAS ORBITTING JUPITER

Shawn L. Bird

"It's not Christmas without a tree, Harvey. I want a Christmas tree."

Colonel Harvey Starman sighed. "Stella. Look around. Where are you going to find a tree?"

Stella scowled. True, Jupiter's moon Titan was a barren place, an endless frozen landscape without any vegetation to speak of, but that didn't mean she couldn't have a Christmas tree. It just meant she had to be creative.

"Be reasonable. Ancient holidays have no place on a colonization mission."

"Celebrations are needed wherever humans are. Traditions bring belonging." Stella pointed, "That triangular antenna is perfect. We'll make decorations that commemorate this beginning. Come."

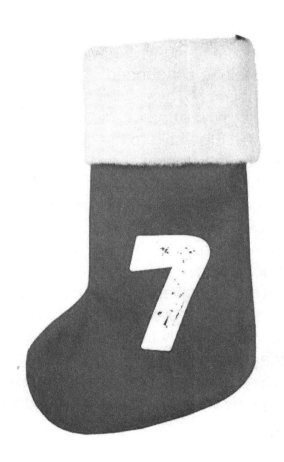

TRADITION BREAKER

Chris McMahen

"There's something wrong with the stuffing," Aunt Penelope announced. "It contains foreign objects."

They're sultana raisins, Aunt Penelope," Elise said to the oldest aunt of her newest husband.

"As I stated…foreign objects," Penelope said. "We are not raisin people, you know. And certainly not in the turkey stuffing. The natural order of the universe does not include raisins in stuffing."

There followed an awkward silence, and Elise knew there was no point in challenging a family tradition that did not include raisins.

She spent the rest of Christmas dinner hoping they wouldn't notice the chocolate filling in the Brussels sprouts.

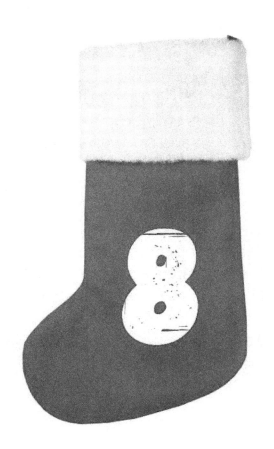

SNOW WAY, JOSÉ

Tim Reynolds

The terrified scream from next door made Zabel nearly drop the big snow shovel.

"José! Stay off the road!"

Zabel was struggling to shovel snow-filled driveways and sidewalks up and down the street instead of Snapchatting with Lisa and was just finishing their own driveway, again.

"Oh my God! José baby! No!"

Hearing the huge approaching snowplow and fearing the worst, Zabel rushed to the end of the driveway just as a snow-covered little black poodle raced around the drift and into her shins, seconds before the plow hammered past. She scooped him up fast. "I got him, Mrs. Garcia!"

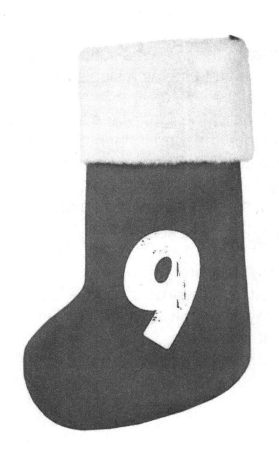

CHRISTMAS TREE

James Bowlby

Decorating the tree was supposed to be fun. It was the first time as a single parent I had to do it alone.

Finally, the lights were strung, the ornaments attached. Laughter echoed as tinsel was flung. Then when it was finished, the lights created their magic.

We had not counted on gravity.

I rushed to grab the falling tree.

There followed a game of holding the tree: my daughter; fixing the tree stand: me.

At last, the tree stood perfectly erect, and we placed gifts lovingly beneath it.

It was ours.

It was beautiful; we could enjoy it.

CHRISTMAS EVE WHITE OUT

Shawn L. Bird

I was a fool to drive through the mountains at night with a blizzard forecast, but I hadn't seen my parents in a year. I wanted to surprise them.

Ha.

A lethal accident wasn't the surprise I'd planned.

I crept forward at 20 km/h. Where was the road?

Headlights flashed behind, and, unbelievably, a semi sped past me. How could it see anything?

I fishtailed as snow splattered my windshield, blinding me.

As the wipers cleared the glass, all I could see were glowing taillights.

I hit the gas, following the lights, my own Bethlehem star guiding me safely home.

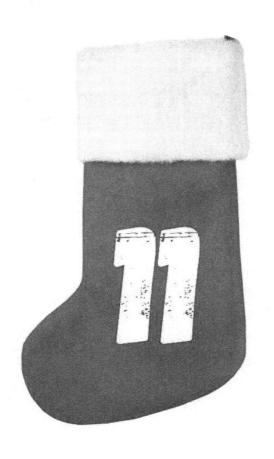

BLACKENED BUTTER TARTS

Finnian Burnett

Smoke from the oven triggers the smoke alarm.

Kevin waves a potholder in the air as Jared races in and turns off the oven. "Kev, what are you doing?"

Kevin collapses against the wall. "Baking," he wails.

Jared's mouth twitches. He grabs the potholder and removes the tray of blackened butter tarts. "They're fine."

"They're ruined." Tears roll down Kevin's face. "I just wanted to impress your family at Christmas dinner."

Jared reaches for a tart from the tray. He blows on it and takes a bite. "Oh, sweetheart. They're already impressed." He swallows the tart and grimaces. "Thank goodness."

NAVIGATION BY WINDROWS AND SNOW RUTS

Carol Parchewsky

He didn't tell me not to take exit 72 seconds before I did.

He didn't tell me I should stop when we passed the eleventh overturned semi in the ditch.

He didn't tell me I didn't know how to drive as I swerved to avoid big horn sheep licking asphalt salt in the middle of the hairpin curve.

He didn't tell me I couldn't have followed the map when we found the ice fortress at the base of Wasetta Falls.

He told me I was the one when we stood under the blazing icicles at sunset in our plaid vests.

THE ETHICAL CHRISTMAS TREE

Chris McMahen

Rubin ordered the tree from ethicaltrees.org sight unseen. It was a Christmas tree with a seal of approval from David Suzuki, Greta Thunberg and Al Gore. The look of the tree was irrelevant. It was environmentally ethical. That's all that mattered.

Three weeks later, a box was delivered to his door by a bicycle courier dressed head to toe in organic hemp. Rubin cut the plant-based adhesive tape with scissors, then lifted the flaps.

There was his tree. Hundreds of multicoloured recycled bread bag fasteners, a ball of twine, and an instruction sheet with only three words:

"Some assembly required."

HOW TO PLAY IN THE SNOW

Finnian Burnett

Reverend Janes watched the women playing in the snow. Grown women; they should be ashamed. They danced and laughed, throwing snowballs.

He had to do something. What would people think?

He stomped into the church yard. "Mrs. Fields," he snapped. "Get ahold of yourself."

She jumped. "My cousin," Mrs. Fields said. "She's never seen snow." She brushed off her coat. "I don't know what came over me."

He looked at the women, standing dejectedly before him. When had he lost his own joy?

Without thinking, he scooped up a pile of snow, flung it, and laughing, ran back to church.

FAMILY RECIPE

Tim Reynolds

Jeff wanted to show his kids that he wasn't nearly as useless as his ex-wife and their mother said, so he called his own mother for the recipe for cookies he cherished at Christmas as a child. Even now he could picture the smudged recipe card propped up on the counter whenever she baked.

"I'm in the store, Mom. What do I need for the secret family cookie recipe?"

"First of all, get the Chipits chocolate chips. Baking Supplies aisle."

He found the chips one aisle over. "Got them."

"Turn the package over."

He did.

"That's the secret family recipe."

IT'S ALL IN THE PACKAGING

Shawn L. Bird

Smoke billowed from the oven.

The gingerbread men were burnt to carbon when Sara pulled them out.

Again.

Third batch.

"If you weren't so busy prepping for the craft sale, you might burn fewer cookies," her mother observed, grabbing one of the trays and bringing it to the table.

"What are you doing?" said Sara as her mom reached for a cellophane bag.

"You can say these are coalminer cookies. You know, they're getting coal in their stocking. A perfect gag gift."

Sara laughed. "Mom, you're a genius."

"I know," chuckled her mom, tying a festive bow on the bag.

WHITE CHRISTMAS OR BUST

Decaying brown grass surrounded the oversized Santa on Sharon's front lawn at the start of December.

The next day she bought a sleigh pulled by racoons. Hank's hardware was sold out of reindeer.

Each successive day without snow Sharon added ornaments: a reindeer stable, a mini-Christmas village, an ostrich family with gold antlers, and even a hot pink pig with silver sequined bows that blinded Karen when she jogged past at noon.

Karen trudged over to complain, crutches barely missing the anchor ropes.

On Christmas Eve, Sharon spray-painted the visible grass arctic white.

The grass was still white in July.

THE TRAIN COMES AND GOES

Finnian Burnett

A whistle wrests me from daydreams of winter travel. Who's taking today's train? Everyone but us.

Dad tries to smile. "I'm sorry we can't go, sweetie."

Our first year missing the family reunion.

I squeeze his hand. "I'd rather be with you."

Another whistle. The train carrying neighbours to far off loved ones.

My dad's lip trembles, but he's distracted by a knock.

A horde of family swarms, carrying suitcases, wrapped presents, food.

My dad's mouth drops. Arms wrap around him, and he blinks, speechless.

"Dad," I say. "We couldn't travel to the family, so the family came to us."

A GAS STATION CHRISTMAS

Chris McMahen

He'd left his shopping late. Appallingly late. All that was open Christmas Eve was the convenience store at the gas bar.

Luckily, he only had to get something for Marnie. She'd done the rest of the shopping for the family.

He decided that this year, he'd go all out and buy Marnie the most expensive thing he could find. He thought about a key chain, but the most expensive one was only $3.95. A $9.99 windshield scraper was a possibility.

But then, he saw it.

Marnie would be blown away by his extravagance! An entire TWELVE PACK of motor oil!

THE PERFECT GIFT

James Bowlby

Giving a gift sure to please is not easy. The purchaser often wants to impress their lover.

Daniel searched the trays of diamond rings for the perfect gift for his wife.

He spotted an understated circle of small diamonds, smooth on the underside, but sparkling. Canadian diamonds. The clerk suggested larger stones, flashier settings. She was sure any woman would want larger, eye-catching diamonds.

But Daniel knew Erin. He didn't want a large, striking ring that would be left in a drawer, but one that suited her and would be worn every day to remind her that he loved her.

SNOW SNAKE CURFEW

Lee F. Patrick

The snow snakes were everywhere this winter, one of the hardest even the elders remembered.

Children were kept in the houses unless they were well bundled. One nip from a snow snake wasn't dangerous for an adult, but for a small child, it might be fatal.

"You're not going out to meet Billy and that's final," Jorie's mother said. "There're snow snakes out. You know what happened to your uncle last winter."

"Some folks don't believe in snow snakes, Mama. They say he was just drunk."

Mama snorted. "It was snow snakes, young lady, and you're staying in until spring."

HOW TO MAKE GINGERBREAD COOKIES FOR SANTA TO GET EXACTLY WHAT YOU ASKED FOR ON SATURDAY AT 2:37 PM AT THE CORNBROOK MALL

Carol Parchewsky

Don't ask Aunt D, she has the wrong cookie cutters, letters, rabbits, and frogs. Why would Santa want a rabbit cookie or the letter W?

Don't ask Aunt J, her oven only knows how to turn cookies blacker than coal.

A haphazard cookie decorated with only eggplant and brown icing results in a pair of navy wool knee highs.

An elegant cookie with the optimum sprinkle to icing to cookie ratio increases the chance of getting the sold out nowhere to be found Hatchimal or such.

Hurry and buy your cookie from Crowmill's Bakery before they close at 4:59 pm.

THE PROMISE

Chris McMahen

Rain fell on Christmas Eve, and Sherman lay wide awake in bed worrying about the ridiculous promise he'd made to the kids. Why promise something completely out of your control? What was he going to tell them when they awoke to disappointment?

At 6:18 am. a loud crash outside woke the household.

Everyone raced to the living room. Through the front window, they saw an overturned semi-truck, its trailer broken open, and millions of tiny foam chips were spilled across their lawn.

"See kids," Sherman said, eyes sparkling. "Didn't I promise you a white Christmas?"

Christmas miracles really do happen.

SNOW ANGELS

Shawn L. Bird

In the morning after each new snowfall, there are snow angels all over the neighbourhood.

They appear in unexpected places, not only in front yards and back yards, but on roofs, on the tops of cars, and the Smith's new RV.

There are no footprints, only a perfectly formed snowy host.

The children are delighted.

Suspicious parents watch nervously out their windows.

Kevin Murphie blogs about aliens.

Little Susie Griffin, just home from the cancer treatment centre, knows the truth, but she isn't telling.

She tracks the iridescent shapes twinkling in lamplight and holds each loved one in her heart.

A MERRY CATMAS

Finnian Burnett

No tree. No presents. Marian's son never asked for anything. Just once, she'd love to give him a real Christmas.

Scratching at the door.

A shivering cat on her stoop.

"I can't feed my family, let alone a stray."

But it whimpered, and she scooped it up.

She fed it and tucked it in. Tomorrow would be better.

In the morning, Tom's yell woke her. "You got me a cat! And a tree!"

Marian rushed downstairs. Tom sat by a decorated tree, cuddling the cat. The stray gave Marian one slow blink and went to sleep in her son's arms.

CAROL PARCHEWSKY

lives in Calgary, Alberta, Canada with her partner and Siberian forest cat. She received her MFA in Fiction from Queens University of Charlotte, her B. Sc. Mechanical Engineering from the University of Saskatchewan. She was the fiction co-editor for QU Literary Magazine.

Carol Parchewsky writes fiction. She is finalizing her novel and working on a collection of short stories. She is President of the WGA. Carol also teaches ESL classes and writing classes.

When she isn't writing or reading, she bakes gingerbread cookies shaped like characters from her stories and she plots how to add more Christmas decorations.

CHRIS MCMAHEN

is the author of four books for young readers. Box of Shocks won the Manitoba Young Readers' Choice Award, while Buddy Concrackle's Amazing Adventure, Klutzhood, and Tabloidology were selected "My Choice" by the Canadian Children's Book Centre. He is a past winner of the Okanagan Short Story and Word on the Lake writing contests. Chris has also written for local theatre groups and published sleep-inducing academic papers. He currently lives in Salmon Arm, British Columbia. In writing Drabbles for this Advent Calendar, his greatest challenge has been to keep the word count of the stories to exactly one…

FINNIAN BURNETT

is a lifelong learner. They're a doctoral student at Murray State University and an MFA instructor with SNHU. Finn has run the Golden Crown Literary Society's Writing Academy since 2015.

Under their former name, Beth Burnett, Finn published several books with Sapphire Publishing. A self-published book, *Coyote Ate the Stars*, won first in fantasy in the Writer's Digest Self-Published Book Awards. They have published in anthologies and journals including *Sinister Wisdom, Flash Fiction magazine,* and *the Resiliency Journal* through the Calgary Arts Development.

Finn lives in the interior of BC with their wife and Lord Gordo, the cat.

JAMES BOWLBY

James's name is associated with theatre, having started Shuswap theatre in 1977. His love of theatre led him to directing many plays.

His writing includes poetry, plays, and short stories, His short story "Agnes Alone" won first prize, 2016 Word on the Lake.

He has just finished the fifth draft of a Youth novel. His wife and daughter are great proofreaders.

A BC guy, he has lived in eight cities, making Salmon Arm his home since 1976. He loves travelling, going across Canada, to Europe and to Egypt twice.

His daughters follow James' interests, Amanda Education; Bronwyn theatre.

LEE F. PATRICK

is a Calgary author writing mostly Science Fiction and Fantasy. Lee has published novels in three different series: *Coalition of Shifters*, *Mind Games*, and *Assassins Justice*. She's also published various short stories and Celtic style poems.

Lee finds it much easier to write a novel than a drabble and has other longer works being released soon.

You can find Lee on Facebook as @LeeFPatrick. All books are available on Amazon and Kobo.

SHAWN L. BIRD

has received award nominations for her darkly humorous novella *Murdering Mr. Edwards* and her YA fantasy series *Grace Awakening.*, She has short-listed or placed in many Canadian short story contests.

She lives in the beautiful Shuswap region of BC where she teaches high school creative writing and lives with her brilliant husband. They have two talented and interesting grown children.

She enjoys wielding needles, plucking strings, collecting amazing footwear, staying up late, and being trained by her miniature poodle.

Visit her blog and book links at www.shawnbird.com. Do check out her Minute Reads and Nikki Knox collections!

TIM REYNOLDS

is a Canadian twistorian, bending and twisting history into fictional shapes for fun. His humorous non-fiction column in SEARCH Magazine is just as entertaining but is based on his bizarre, event-filled life.

Tim's 100-word story "Temper Temper" was a winner of Kobo Writing Life's Jeffrey Archer Short Story Challenge, and his short story "Tamarack and the Stone" was a finalist for the 2016 Baen Fantasy Adventure Award. Originally from Toronto, Tim now resides in Calgary, Alberta, writing novels and arguing with his cats and dog about which one gets to be the hero of the next great story.

If you enjoyed this book, please leave a review on the retail site where you purchased it and/or on a review site like Goodreads. Thank you!

**Merry Christmas
and
Happy New Year to you!**

~THE END~

CPSIA information can be obtained
at www.ICGtesting.com
Printed in the USA
BVHW050530110921
616350BV00003B/16